# MY BIG BROTHER

By Miriam Cohen

Art by Ronald Himler

Published in the United States of America by Star Bright Books, Inc.,
13 Landsdowne Street, Cambridge, MA 02139.

The name Star Bright Books and the Star Bright Books logo are registered
trademarks of Star Bright Books, Inc.

Please visit www.starbrightbooks.com. For bulk orders, please email: orders@starbrightbooks.com,
or call customer service at: (617) 354-1300.

Hardcover ISBN: 978-1-59572-007-8
Star Bright Books / MA / 00404110
Printed in China (WKT) 0 9 8 7 6 5 4

Paperback ISBN: 978-1-59572-158-7
Star Bright Books / MA / 00306130
Printed in China (WKT) 0 9 8 7 6 5 4 3

Printed on paper from sustainable forests.

Library of Congress Cataloging-in-Publication Data

Cohen, Miriam.
  My big brother / by Miriam Cohen ; art by Ronald Himler.
    p. cm.
  Summary: When his big brother leaves to become a soldier, a boy does what he can to take
his place in the family.
  ISBN 1-59572-007-3
  [1. Brothers--Fiction. 2. Family life--Fiction. 3. Soldiers--Fiction.] I. Himler, Ronald, ill. II. Title.

PZ7.M6628My 2004
[E]--dc22
                          2004016056

This is me and my big brother.

My big brother plays basketball.
He jumps up in the sky —
and the ball goes right in the basket!

He holds me up so I can do it.
The ball goes right in the basket.
"Good shot, little brother!"

He is really smart.
He reads lots of books and
sometimes he reads to me.

This is a picture of my big brother and me when I was little. I'm not *really* playing the music.

On Saturday we go to the "Making Our Neighborhood Better" meeting, and Mama puts on her nice hat.
My big brother says, "Mama, you look pretty."

After the meeting we have dinner.
We have pot roast and gravy, potatoes,
and pudding with whipped cream
twirled on top.

My big brother says, "Thank you, Mama."

My big brother has an old car.
He likes to fix it on the weekend.
He always lets me help.

My big brother is really smart, but college costs a lot.
So he is going into the army.

Mama says, "Take your warm socks!"

I make a card and give it to him.

"You are the big brother now," he says.
"You take care of our family."

I tell him, "I will!"

Now I hold up *my* little brother.
He drops the ball right in the basket.
"Good shot, little brother!" I say.

We wash our big brother's car every weekend.
I give my little brother a sponge.
"We have to keep big brother's car nice for him," I tell him.

Mama puts on her nice hat for the neighborhood meeting.
I say, "Mama, you look really pretty."
"I like that hat," says my little brother.

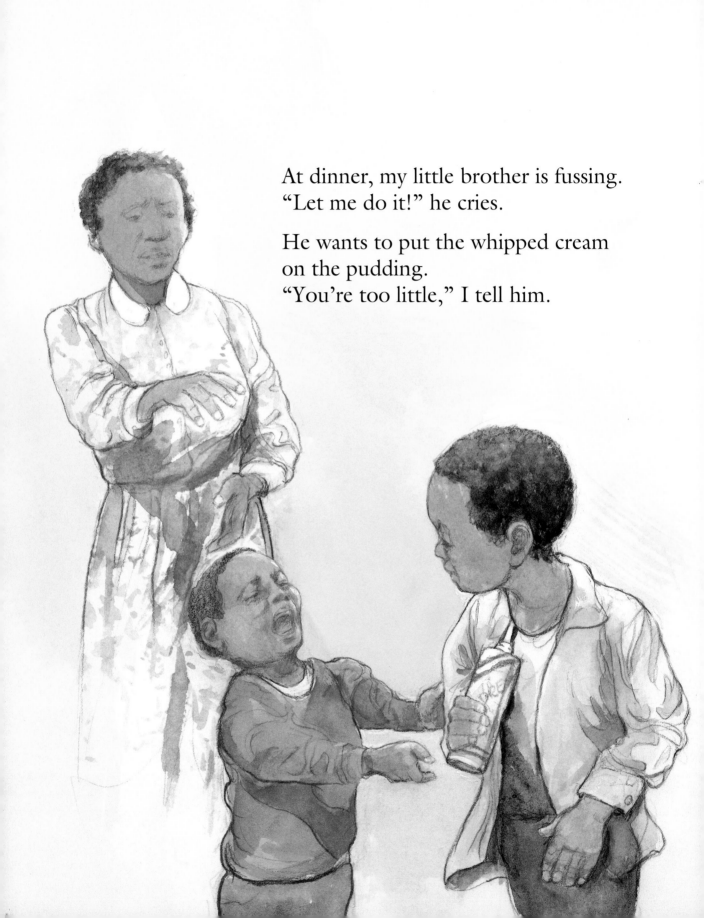

At dinner, my little brother is fussing.
"Let me do it!" he cries.

He wants to put the whipped cream
on the pudding.
"You're too little," I tell him.

But then I remember –
I'm the big brother now.
I help my little brother hold the can.
He puts a lot of whipped cream
on the pudding.

At night we watch the news on TV.
Maybe we'll see our big brother.

Tears come in Mama's eyes.
She says, "I know what we'll do."

"We'll bake his favorite cookies and send them to him in the army."

I write a letter to go with the cookies.

My big brother sent us a picture.
It said, "To my family, with all my love."
We look at it a lot.

I keep my big brother's car shiny for him.

I miss him.